First Paperback Edition 1994

Text and illustrations copyright © 1992 by Martina Selway

Published by Ideals Children's Books
Nashville, Tennessee

First published in Great Britain by
Hutchinson Children's Books, an imprint of the
Random Century Group, Ltd., London, England

Printed in China.

Library of Congress Cataloging-in-Publication Data

Selway, Martina
    Don't forget to write/ written and illustrated by Martina Selway.
        p.   cm.
    Summary: As she adds to the letter she is writing home, Rosie
expresses her changing feelings about her visit to her
grandfather's farm.
    ISBN 0-8249-8543-5 (trade)—ISBN 0-8249-8636-9 (paper)
    [1. Separation anxiety—Fiction. 2. Grandfathers—Fiction.
3. Farm life—Fiction.] I. Title
PZ7.S4624Do   1991
[E]—dc20   91-28430
                                                              CIP
                                                               AC

Don't Forget to Write

Martina Selway

Ideals Children's Books
Nashville, Tennessee

For Rosemary Davidson

"I don't want to stay with Grandad and Aunty Mabel," Rosie said. "I don't like smelly farms. I won't have anyone to play with. I want to stay at home!"

"Come on, Rosie," Mom answered. "Grandad and Aunty Mabel haven't seen you in ages. You'll love all the animals, and you'll have lots of fun.

"Now don't forget to take baths, don't forget to wash your hair, don't forget to brush your teeth, and ... don't forget to write."

Griggs Farm,
Manchester,
Vermont.

Dear Mom,
    I didn't want you to leave me at
Grandad's. When you left, I cried
and cried.
Grandad said, "Come on Old Ginger
Nut, dry those tears and let's
see if Aunty Mabel has made us
a snack."
I don't like being called "Old Ginger Nut."
I want to come home.

Bess and Rags barked and jumped and licked me all over. Aunty Mabel told me not to cuddle the dogs because they have fleas.

Grandad said, "Don't be ridiculous. A few fleas never hurt anybody."

I don't want to get fleas.

I want to come home.

Aunty Mabel made some toast on the fire and I had one of her special raisin cookies. It was very hard.

Grandad said, "Don't drop it on the floor. It'll crack the tiles."

My wobbly tooth came out.

I want to come home.

When it was time for bed, Aunty Mabel wrapped up my tooth and put it under my pillow for the tooth fairy.

Grandad said, "We haven't had the tooth fairy here in years. I hope she finds the way."

How will she know I'm staying at Grandad's?

I wish I were at home.

The fairy came! She left me some money, but there are no stores for me to buy anything.

Grandad said, "We're going to town on Tuesday; it'll have to burn a hole in your pocket till then."
I could have gone to the mini-market on my roller skates if I were at home.

I helped Aunty Mabel collect
eggs from all over the farm. She
told me to look in all the dark and
cozy places.
I found a rat's nest in the hay barn.
Grandad said, "Darn pests. They're
a darn nuisance."
I'd like a pet rat when I get home.

After dinner I explored in Grandad's big
cabinets. There was so much to look at
that I stayed up really late.
I told Grandad that I was searching
for buried treasure.
Grandad said, "You're just like your Mom,
Old Ginger Nut, silly as a goose."
I found some funny old pictures of you.
I can bring them with me when I come home.

Grandad took me fishing in the river
this afternoon. I waited for ages and
ages but he didn't catch a fish.
I got fed up and made a dam
with the stones.
Grandad said, "Just hold your horses,
we'll have a fish as big as a whale
in a minute."
Aunty Mabel cooked fish sticks for dinner.
I wish we had a river at home.

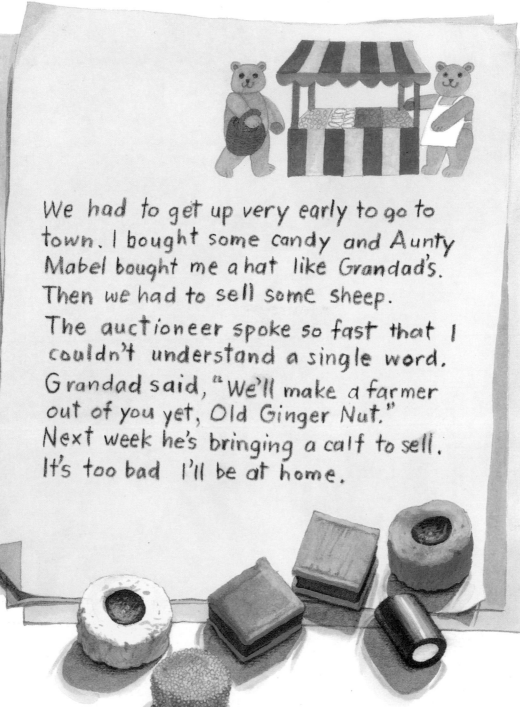

We had to get up very early to go to town. I bought some candy and Aunty Mabel bought me a hat like Grandad's.

Then we had to sell some sheep.

The auctioneer spoke so fast that I couldn't understand a single word.

Grandad said, "We'll make a farmer out of you yet, Old Ginger Nut."

Next week he's bringing a calf to sell. It's too bad I'll be at home.

Aunty Mabel made us a picnic today because we had a long climb up the hill to fetch the sheep. It was very hot. All we could hear were sheep munching grass and bees buzzing.
Grandad said, "It's going to be a lot quieter next week without you buzzing around!"
I can't believe there are only two days left before I have to come home.

Grandad said, "It's time we mailed that letter. I thought you were writing a book, it's taken you so long!"
PLEASE let me stay a little longer with Grandad.
I don't want to come home yet.
Lots of love,
Old Ginger Nut. X

Ms. A. Lee
1764 Hill Road
Hartford, Connecticut.

fish

look

roller
~~ders~~ sckates